BANANAS are not the only Fruit

David Shenton

ACKNOWLEDGEMENTS
These cartoons first appeared in Capital Gay, The Guardian, Vada, Forum, Him and City Limits.
With thanks to Michael Mason, Bob Workman and Tony.

© 1993 David Shenton

All rights reserved. No part of this publication may be reproduced stored in a retrieval system, or transmitted in any form or by any means, electronic, mechanical, photocopying, recording or otherwise, without the prior permission of the copyright owner.

Published by Stonewall Press

Printed in Great Britian

ISBN 0 95 22024 0 9

Once upon a time....

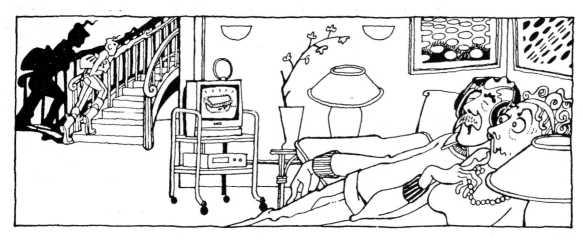

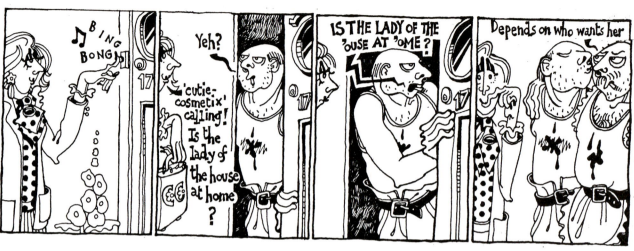

lovely pedalbins...

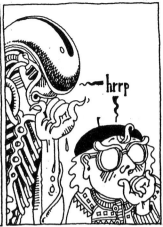

200,000 legs

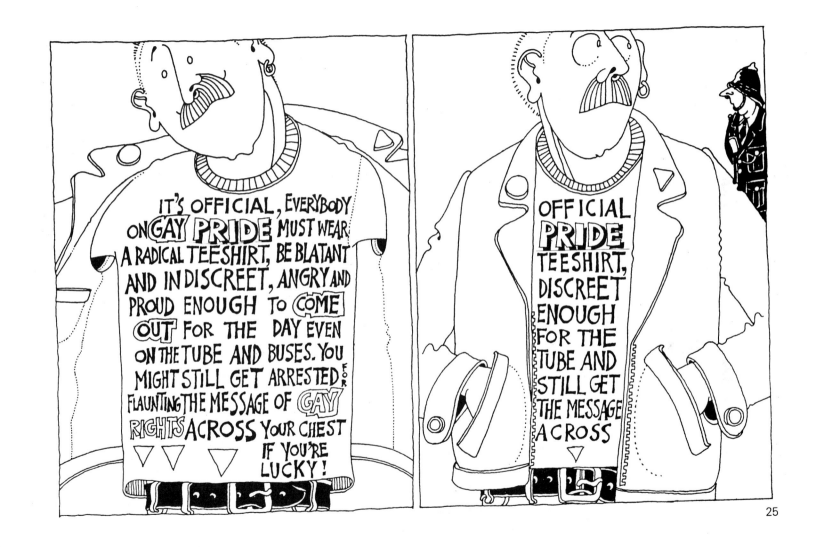

THING..

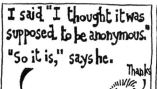

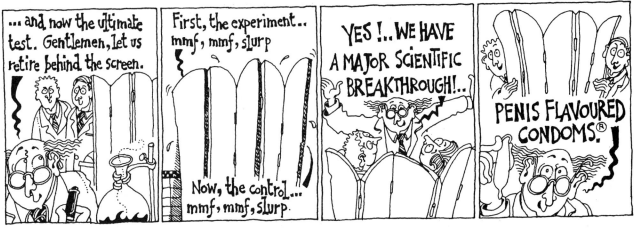

'Cuddle a Clone for Christmas'

Good morning. I represent the 'Cuddle a Clone for Christmas Appeal' and I have a selection of specialized items that might appeal to a man of taste such as yourself.

① A voice-operated S+M Advent Calendar that only opens its little doors if you say please,..

② A novelty flashlight in the shape of a beckoning finger that hooks onto your belt to show exactly what colour hanky you're sporting, even in the darkest club,..

and ③ Hand-picked jock straps worn by the raunchier shepherds from the Bethlehem catchment area for 40 days and 40 nights. — Fittings available on request.

You'd better come in.

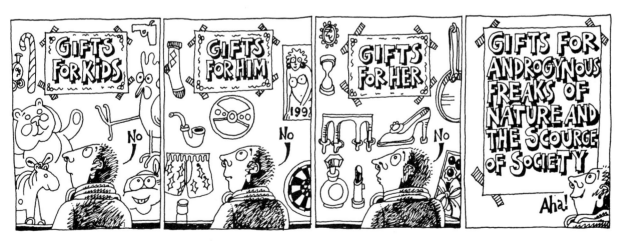

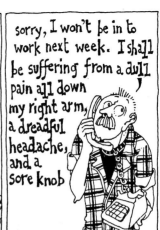

Fondue Set

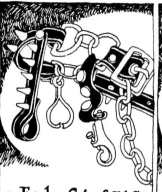  

1. Garlic Press £17·95   2. Fondue Set £34·50   3. Pastry Aerator £31·95

Mrs Harris, our top designer for 25 years, and she still thinks it's kitchenware!

BADMINTON HORSe TRJALS...

The accused was seen to approach his victim... S+M NOW A CRIME

..in the sordid dinginess of the homosexual underworld and was distinctly heard to whisper:-

"I'D LIKE TO WHISK YOU OFF"!

now m'lud doesn't need the morals of St. Cecilia to know this practise is NOT NATURAL!

Throughout Britain, Lord Lane's ruling is causing havoc in the nation's sex dungeons SLING! JUNCTION!

RACK! GOODS DEPOT! ...as more and more members of the leather community

..see it as an ideal opportunity to convert the space into layouts for their... FLOGGING POST!!

trainsets SHUNTING YARD!

Tender Dark Places

A SHORT GUIDE TO THE SOL BOTTLE CODE...

1. LIME angled to the left

passive straight-acting with an amazing collection of 'Les Mis' CDs in the Toyota

2. sickly choc / alka seltzer

hyper active fun loving bubbly Su Pollard devotee (or indeed the lovely Su herself)

3. grubby jock / is this really sol?...or a similar amber liquid?

rather shocking leather man public demonstrating his proclivities in the hope of appearing in the press or a slot on Channel 4's 'OUT'

cork / have you seen the price of this stuff?

me

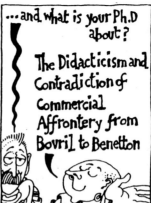

Wild Latin Rhythms

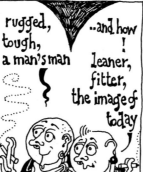

unsavoury aspects

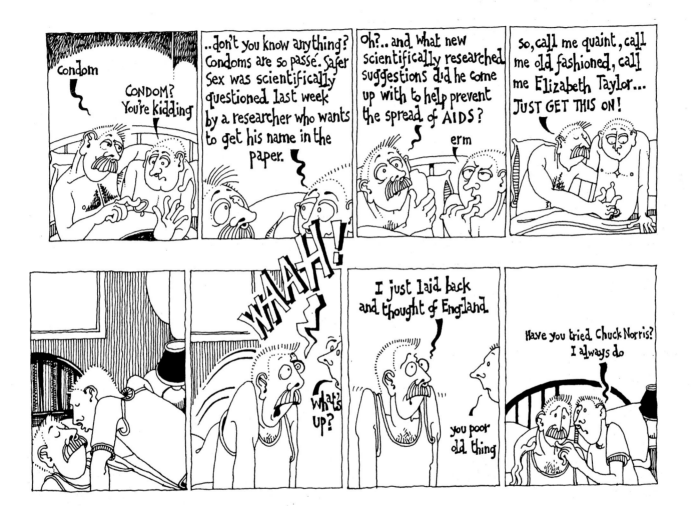

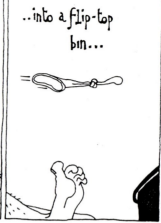

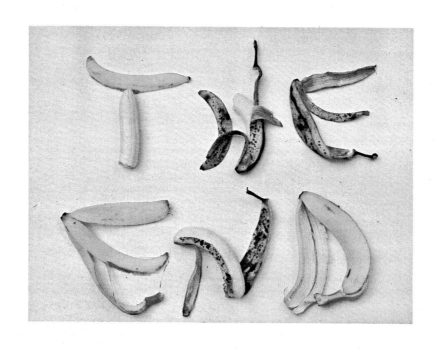